Goldilocks
and the Three Bears

As Told By Pam Tillis

Illustrated by Jane Chambless Wright

A Byron Preiss Book

Dutton Children's Books
New York

Published in the United States by Dutton Children's Books,

a division of Penguin Young Readers Group

345 Hudson Street, New York, New York 10014

www.penguin.com

Manufactured in China

10 9 8 7 6 5 4 3 2 1

First Edition

ISBN 0-525-47153-7

For the Goldilocks in all of us

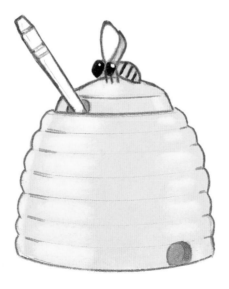

ONCE UPON A TIME there were three bears. There was Big Old Daddy Bear, a big old furry guy who could get kind of grumpy and gruff, especially when he was hungry. But everybody who knew him said he was just a big old teddy bear with a heart of honey.

Then there was Sweet Middle-Sized Mama Bear. She was a kindly kind of bear, real good-natured, always humming a tune.

And of course, there was Little Bitty Baby Bear. He was a cute little furry guy with a bubbly personality, but he could get a tad whiny, especially when he was tired.

The three bears lived in a comfy country cabin in the foothills of the Smoky Mountains. They had it fixed up real homey, with ruffled curtains on the windows, antiques handed down from Sweet Mama Bear's great-grand-daddy, and a wood-burning stove, just right for those frosty winter nights. It wasn't fancy, but it sure was home.

Great Grand-Daddy "Lucky"

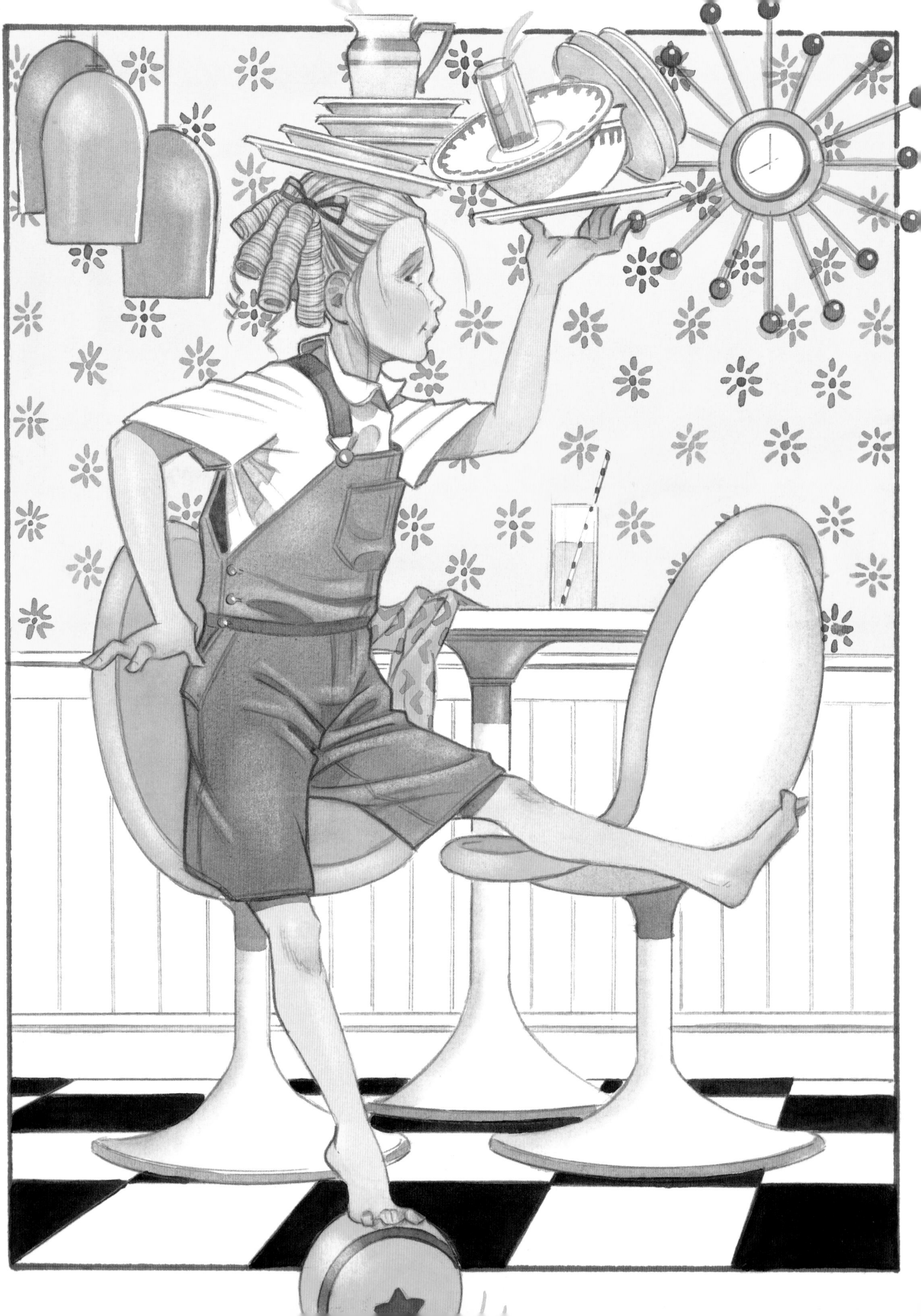

Now, down the road a ways lived a little curly-headed girl named Goldilocks. Goldilocks was always getting into everything. Her mama said she was full of mischief, and it's true—sometimes Goldilocks's curiosity got the best of her.

Well, one morning, Goldilocks asked her mama if she could go out and play. Her mama said, "Sure, hon, but don't wander too far away from the house. Remember, there're bears out back in the woods."

"Okay, Mama," answered Goldilocks. But, being the feisty kind of girl she was, she didn't always mind her mama, and on this particular morning she set off straight for the woods.

That Goldilocks climbed a tree, walked on some logs, looked for some frogs, and before she knew it, she was way out in the woods. Farther than she'd ever been before.

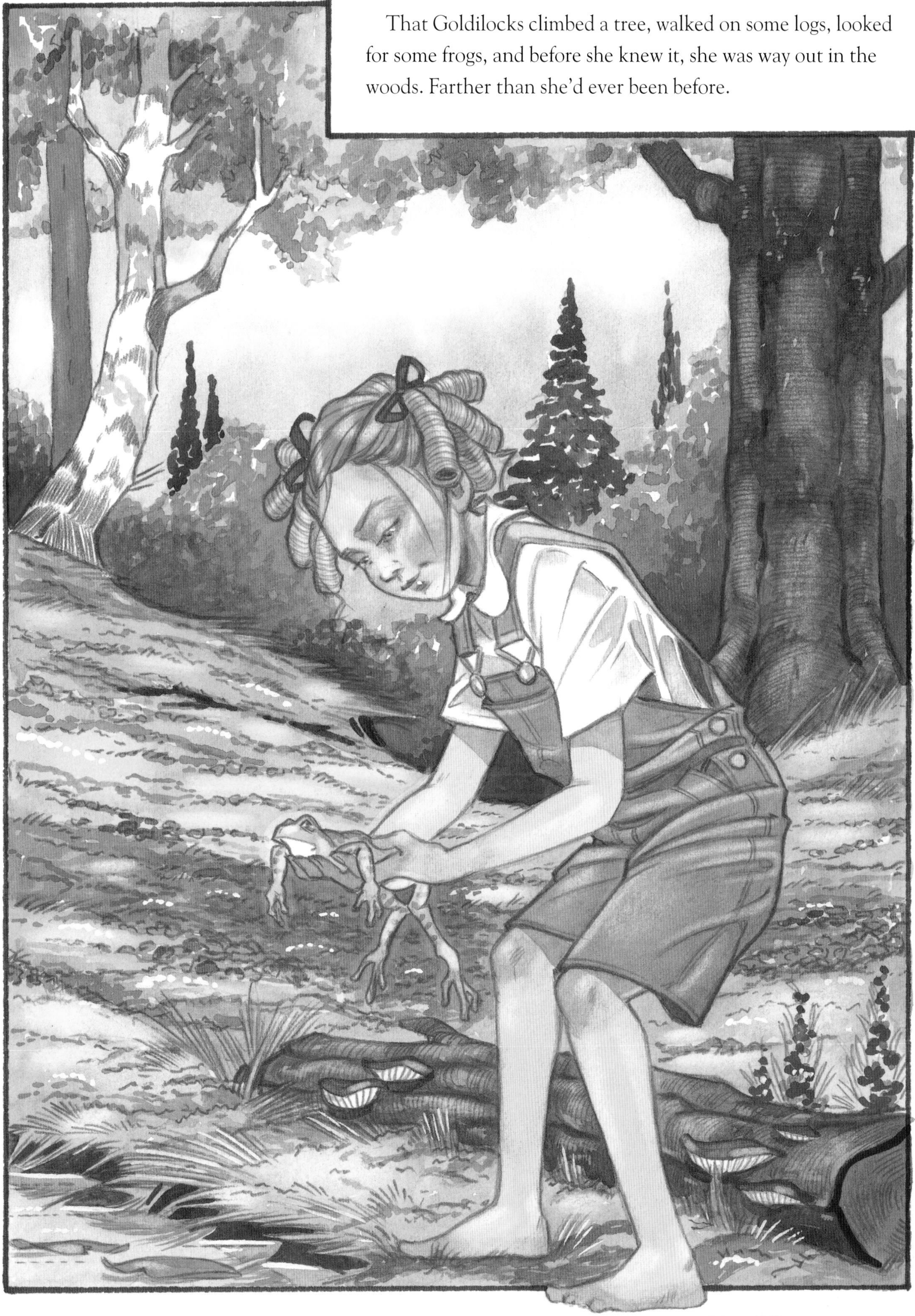

Right about now the three bears were fixing to sit down to breakfast. "Breakfast is ready, y'all," said Sweet Mama Bear.

"It's a good thing, 'cause I'm hungry," grumbled Big Old Daddy Bear.

"Yay! Porridge!" said Little Bitty Baby Bear.

Big Old Daddy Bear sat down at the kitchen table in front of his big old bowl of porridge. Sweet Mama Bear sat down in front of her middle-sized bowl of porridge, and Little Bitty Baby Bear sat down in front of his little bitty bowl of porridge.

"This porridge is way too hot!" growled Big Old Daddy Bear.

"It is a bit hot, isn't it?" said Sweet Mama Bear.

"Waah! I burned my tongue!" cried Little Bitty Baby Bear. He could get kind of whiny when he was upset.

"Why don't we go down to the pond for a few minutes and try to catch some catfish while our porridge is cooling down?" said Big Old Daddy Bear.

"Good idea," said Sweet Mama Bear.

"Yay! Catfish!" said Little Bitty Baby Bear.

So they headed out the back door and down to the pond.

Meanwhile, Goldilocks had come to a little clearing in the woods and, to her surprise, saw the three bears' comfy country cabin. "What in the world is this?" said Goldilocks to nobody in particular as she ran down the path to get a good look. She peeked in through the ruffled curtains.

"This sure is a pretty little place, but I don't see anybody in there." Goldilocks went on over to the front door and knocked. *Hmm,* she thought to herself, *they probably wouldn't mind if I went on in. I just love looking at houses.* Goldilocks was hoping to be an interior designer when she grew up.

Getting no answer at the door, Goldilocks turned the doorknob and went on inside. Now, I don't believe I'd be going inside somebody's house if they didn't answer, would you? But that's just the kind of girl Goldilocks was, full of mischief.

"Yum! Smells like breakfast!" said Goldilocks as she walked on over to the table where the three bears' breakfast was cooling down. "I think I'll have me some," she said.

Goldilocks sat down in front of Big Old Daddy Bear's big old bowl of porridge and dug right in. "Yuck! This is too salty!" said Goldilocks. Old Daddy Bear did like to use a whole lot of salt, something Sweet Mama Bear had been getting on him about lately.

Then Goldilocks moved on over to Sweet Mama Bear's middle-sized bowl of porridge and took a taste of it. "Ewww! Too sweet!!" she said. That Sweet Middle-Sized Mama Bear did like a touch too much honey every now and then.

So Goldilocks slid on over to Little Bitty Baby Bear's little bitty bowl of porridge. "Mmmm! Not too salty, not too sweet, this is just right!" And she ate it all up.

Well, Goldilocks figured she'd have a look around the place, seeing as how no one was at home.

"Sure is quiet in here. How about some music?" she said, and she walked over to the three bears' radio and turned it on.

Then Goldilocks saw three chairs in the living room and plopped right down in Daddy Bear's big old recliner. "Yeeow! What is this?" Big Old Daddy Bear's remote control was poking into her arm. Goldilocks flipped back the recliner and almost fell over backward trying to get out.

"That chair was way too hard," she said, and she headed for Sweet Mama Bear's middle-sized chair, which was covered with soft cushions.

Goldilocks sat down in the chair. "Yeow! Not again!" One of Sweet Mama Bear's knitting needles poked right into Goldilocks's leg.

"This chair's way too squishy for me," she said as she pulled herself up and climbed over the side.

Then she saw Little Bitty Baby Bear's little bitty rocking chair. "Oh, how cute! I need to try this one out." Goldilocks sat down and said, "This chair's not too hard, and it's not too squishy—it's just right!" And she started to rock and rock, faster and faster, just having the best old time.

Well, Goldilocks was about to set the world's record for speed rocking when all of a sudden the arms came loose, the legs came loose, and the bottom came slap out of that rocking chair. Goldilocks landed flat as a fritter on her backside.

"Good grief! They sure don't make rockers like they used to," complained Goldilocks as she got up and brushed herself off.

Uncle Gladly

Ursa Major

Ursa Minor

Cousin
Fuzzy · Wuzzy

Now, all this rocking had made Goldilocks downright sleepy, so she thought she'd look for a place to take a little nap. She spied a stairway with an oak railing. *What a great sliding banister,* thought Goldilocks as she climbed up to the three bears' bedroom.

When she reached the top of the stairs and saw the three beds, Goldilocks had a sudden burst of energy. "What great beds for jumping!"

Goldilocks ran right over to Big Old Daddy Bear's big old bed and hopped on. The bed didn't have any bounce to it at all. "This bed's way too hard," said Goldilocks as she jumped off.

Next she saw Sweet Mama Bear's middle-sized bed, covered with a lovely patchwork quilt. Goldilocks knew her mama wouldn't think much of her bouncing on such a pretty bed that was all made up, but being the feisty kind of girl Goldilocks was, she went ahead and bounced on it anyway.

Goldilocks sunk way down in the mattress. Being full of feathers and down, it didn't have any bounce to it either. "This bed's way too soft," said Goldilocks, and she slowly rolled out.

"I guess I'll try out that cute little bed over there," she said as she hopped on over to Little Bitty Baby Bear's little bitty bed. "This bed isn't too hard, and it isn't too soft—it's just right!"

And Goldilocks bounced and rolled this-a-way and that-a-way until she just wore herself out! *Yawn.* "I'm sleepy," said Goldilocks as she snuggled underneath Baby Bear's cozy comforter. And before she knew it, she fell fast asleep and drifted right off into dreamland.

Figuring their porridge had cooled by now, the three bears headed back to the house and straight for the kitchen table.

"Somebody's been into my porridge," grumbled Big Old Daddy Bear with his big old grumpy voice. "Why, somebody's been into my porridge, too," said Sweet Middle-Sized Mama Bear with her sweet middle-sized voice. "Somebody's been into my porridge, and they ate it all up!" whined Little Bitty Baby Bear. "WAAH!!"

Right then, Big Old Daddy Bear heard music coming from the other room and headed in there to check it out.

It didn't take him but a second to see that somebody had moved his recliner. "Somebody's been sitting in my chair and messing with the remote," growled Big Old Daddy Bear. He was really starting to get grouchy now.

Sweet Middle-Sized Mama Bear noticed that her knitting needles were out of place. "It looks like somebody's been sitting in my chair, too," she said, sounding kind of puzzled.

"Somebody's been sitting in my chair and busted it all to pieces," whined Little Bitty Baby Bear. "WAAH!!"

Big Old Daddy Bear started up the stairs to the three bears' bedroom. "Y'all wait here while I take a look upstairs." But by the time Big Old Daddy Bear had reached the top of the stairs, the other two bears were right behind him.

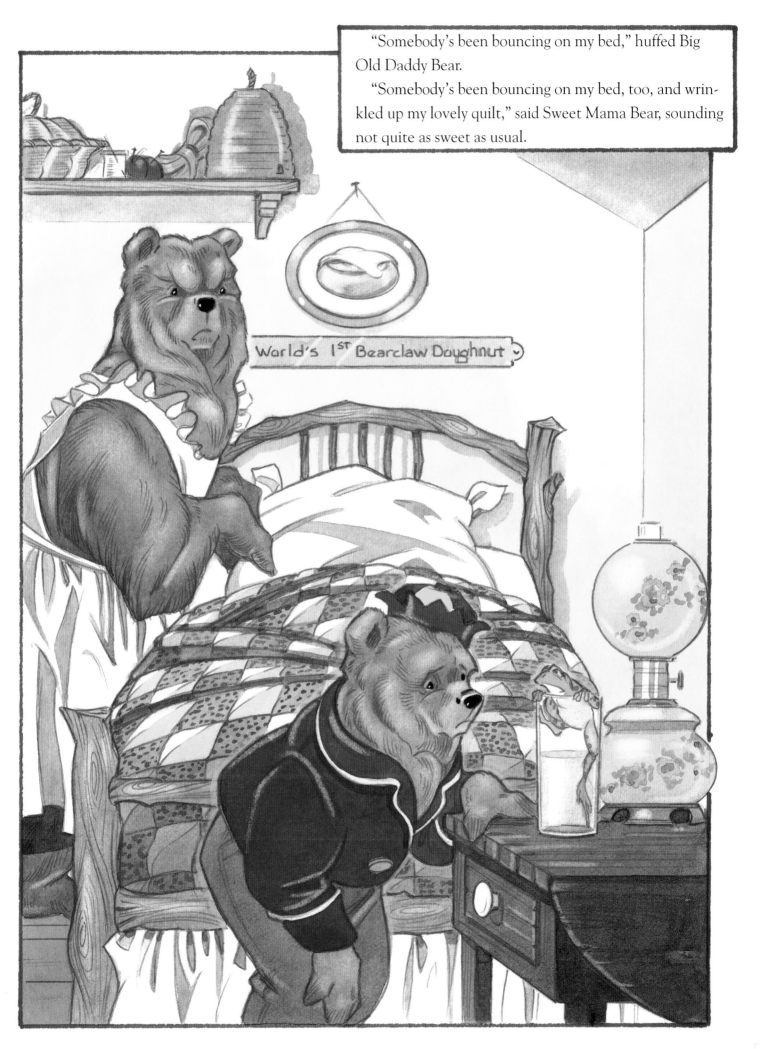

"Somebody's been bouncing on my bed," huffed Big Old Daddy Bear.

"Somebody's been bouncing on my bed, too, and wrinkled up my lovely quilt," said Sweet Mama Bear, sounding not quite as sweet as usual.

"Somebody's been sleeping in my bed and she's still here! WAAAH!!"

When Little Bitty Baby Bear got really upset, his shrill voice sounded just like a siren, and it scared Goldilocks right out of her sleep. Goldilocks saw the three bears standing there and let out a shriek. "AAAH!!"

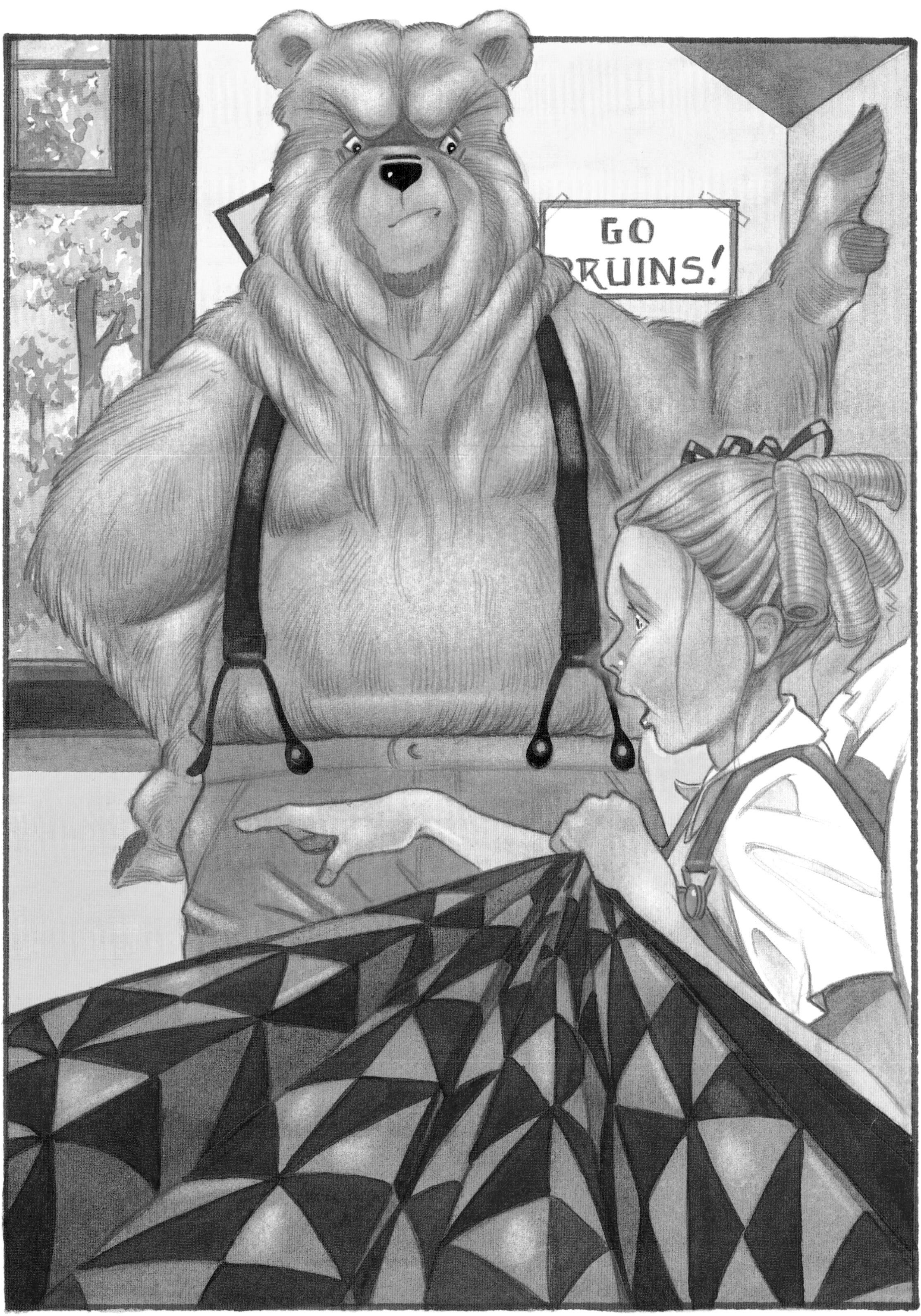
GO
RUINS!

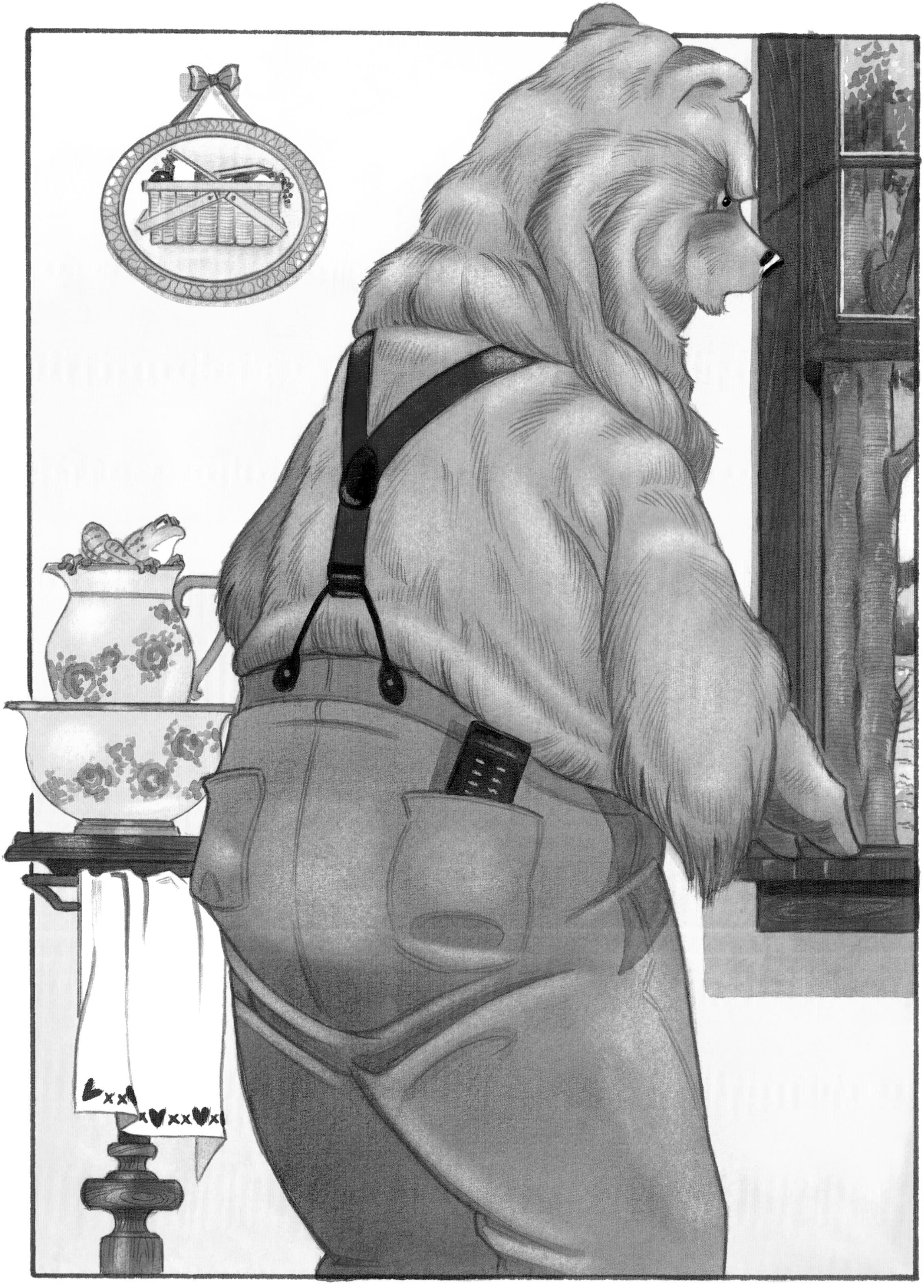

She jumped out of bed, climbed out the window, and slid down the tree outside. She ran all the way home, crying, "Mama, Mama, I'm gonna mind you from now on!"

"Come see us sometime!" hollered Sweet Middle-Sized Mama Bear.

"Bless her heart, we must've scared her," said Big Old Daddy Bear.

"Mama, I'm still hungry," said Little Bitty Baby Bear. Since by now their porridge was cold and ruined, Sweet Mama Bear said, "How about we fix us a nice breakfast of sausage and biscuits?"

"Yay! Biscuits!" said Little Bitty Baby Bear.

"Well, it's a shame that little girl's gonna miss out on all this good food," said Big Old Daddy Bear as they headed for the kitchen.

"Maybe she'll come back and play sometime," said Little Bitty Baby Bear.

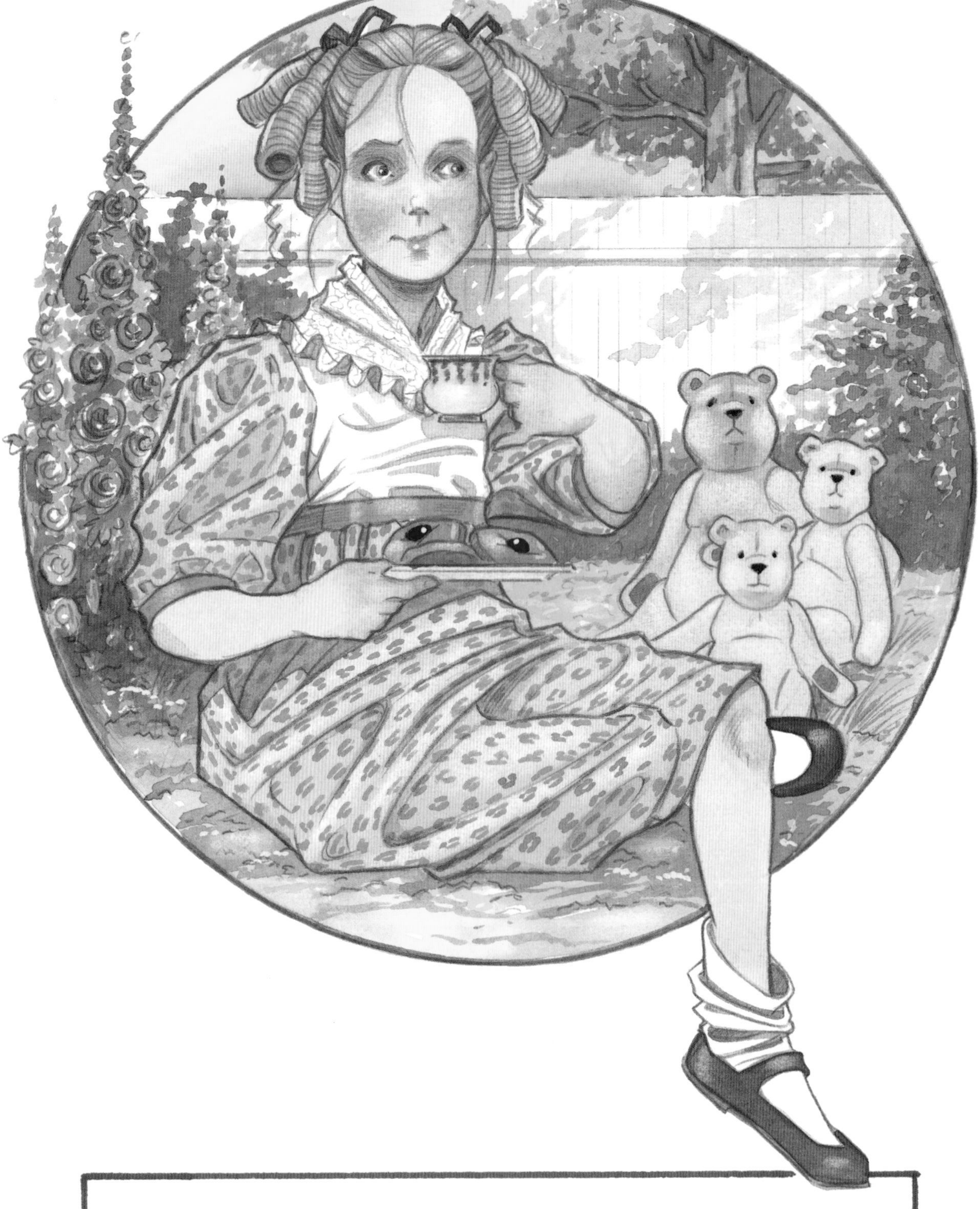

But you know what? Goldilocks never did come back. 'Cause even though the three bears were mighty nice and Goldilocks liked to make all kinds of new friends, she decided it would probably be a pretty good idea to mind her mama. So from that day on, Goldilocks always let her mama know where she was headed before she went anywhere. As a matter of fact, for a while anyway, Goldilocks didn't even want to wander off into the woods. Not one little bit. She liked staying right at home.